Another Point of View

Giants Have Feelings, Too

by Dr. Alvin Granowsky
illustrations by Henry Buerchkholtz

I am sure that the rest of you people living down below are very nice. But that boy, Jack, is something else. After I was so kind to him, he stole from us, and he hurt my husband. All because we are giants! That's no reason to take our treasures or to make my husband fall on his head. See what you think.

The first time I set eyes on the boy, he was at my front door. He looked so thin and hungry. So of course, I invited him in and gave him something to eat. I do love to cook, you know. Herbert, my husband, just loves my cooking.

It warmed my heart to watch that boy enjoy the meal I made. Jack was still eating when Herbert's footsteps shook the room. Jack jumped into the oven to hide.

I should have known right then that Jack was up to no good. I just thought the boy was shy. But he wasn't shy about taking what he wanted!

I thought Herbert would meet Jack after we ate. I knew Herbert would love to get to know the boy. You see, our five sons are grown. We do miss having children around.

After the last bite of our tasty meal, Herbert asked for our bags of gold. He keeps a close eye on our savings. We have to save up for the day when we can't work.

Counting those coins made Herbert a bit tired. Soon his snores were shaking the room.

"Oh, dear!" I thought. "Herbert hasn't met Jack yet. Well, Jack will just have to wait until Herbert wakes up." Just then, I heard the front door slam. "That's funny," I thought. But I went on with my work and truly, I forgot about Jack. I didn't think anymore about him until later.

When Herbert woke up, he called, "Dear, did you move our bags of gold?"

"No, dear," I answered.

"Well, I can't find them," he said.

"Before the day is over, you'll trip over them somewhere," I laughed. But we never saw those bags of gold again.

Herbert and I were raised not to think badly about others, but I couldn't help wondering about Jack. Why had he left without saying goodbye? Did he know something about our gold?

In time, I forgot about the boy's visit. Then one morning, who should I see at my front door but Jack. He didn't look quite as hungry as the last time, but he said he was. Again, I let him in.

"Did you happen to come across a couple bags of gold on your last visit?" I asked.

"Let me think," Jack answered. "Some of your wonderful homemade bread might help me remember."

I must say I was pleased. My bread has won blue ribbons, but I don't really tell anybody about that.

Before we could talk anymore about the missing gold, the room began to shake.

"Oh, good. You'll get to meet my Herbert," I said.

"I'll meet him after he eats," Jack said as he jumped into the oven.

"Well, that will be fine," I said. I thought to myself, "That boy is a little too shy for his own good."

Then Herbert came in singing, "Fe! Fi! Fo! Fum! My wife's cooking is *Yum! Yum! Yum!* Be it baked or be it fried, we finish each meal with her tasty pies!"

"Oh, Herbert," I laughed. He does like my pies. They have won some blue ribbons, too, but I really don't ever tell anybody about that.

Herbert ate the last crumb on his plate. Then he went to get our pet hen. She lays eggs of solid gold. "Our little hen helps us save for the future," Herbert said.

He had the hen lay one egg and then another. Soon Herbert's snores shook the room.

I forgot about Jack being in the oven until I heard the front door slam. When I looked out the window, I saw Jack running off with our hen.

By the time I woke up Herbert, Jack was long gone.

"That boy's been here before," I cried. "He must be the one who took our gold. And now he's taken our hen!"

"Oh, dear," Herbert said. "We can only hope that the boy's mother will find out what he has done. Surely, she will make him return our things. Maybe she will even return them herself."

"You're right, Herbert," I said. "When his mother brings back our gold and our hen, I'll be here to thank her."

"Don't worry," Herbert added. "Everything will work out for the best."

Well, someone did come back, but not to return what was ours. Jack came back to take the last of our treasures. This time, though, he got into the house without our knowing about it.

Herbert and I were listening to our lovely golden harp. Then Herbert began to snore, and I left the room.

Suddenly, our harp cried out, "Help, Master! I am being stolen!"

I rushed back into the room and saw Jack. He was running out the front door and taking our harp with him.

"Get up, Herbert!" I yelled.

"Stop! You're stealing!" Herbert yelled as he ran after Jack. "Don't you know it's wrong to steal?"

Jack just ran faster. Then he started to climb down that beanstalk.

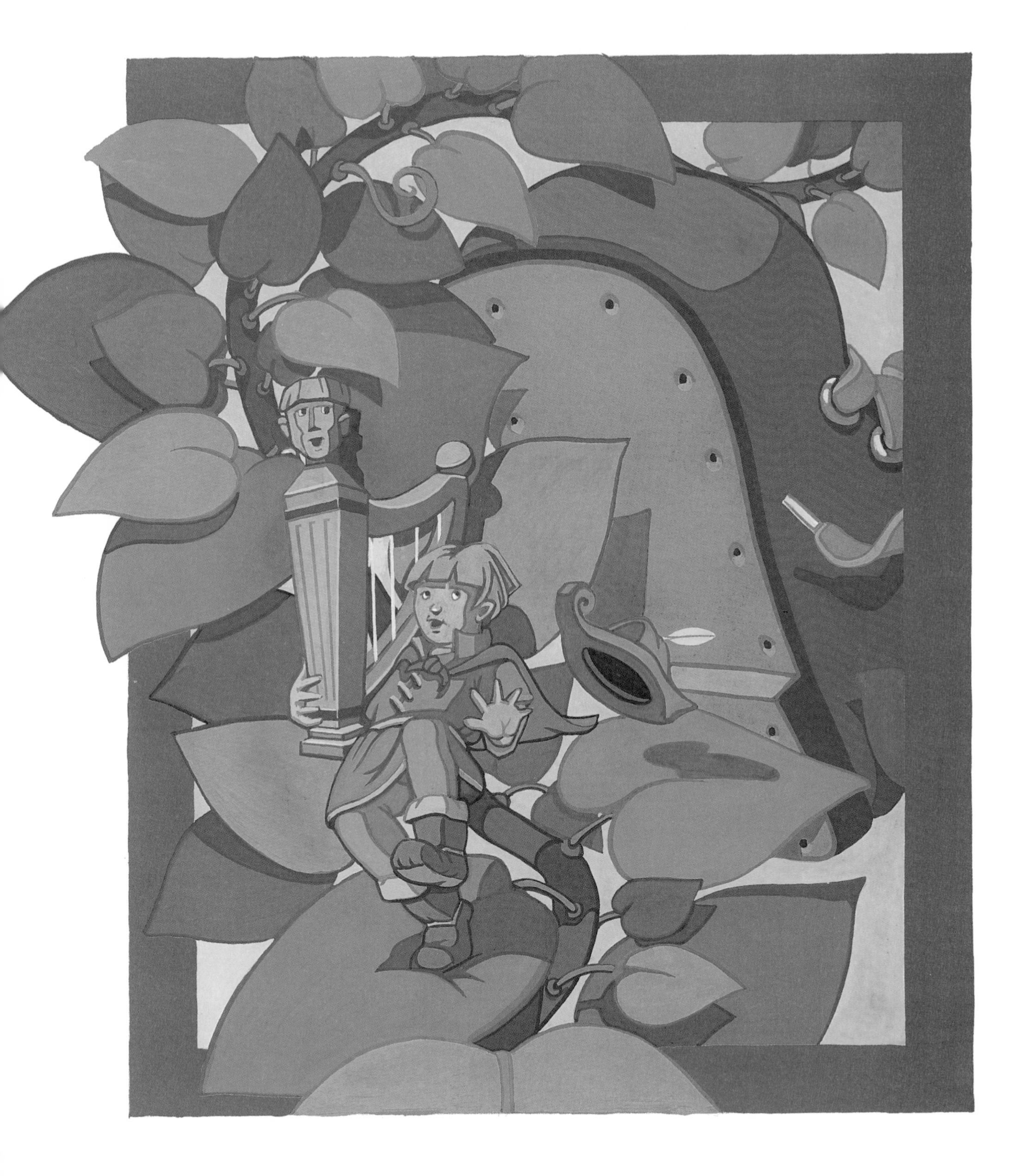

"Be careful!" I called to Herbert as he started down the beanstalk. "It's a long way to the ground below!"

Then I heard chopping sounds. I looked down and saw Jack swinging an ax.

The beanstalk fell to the ground, and my poor husband took a nasty fall. Thank goodness Herbert has a hard head!

Now we hear that Jack and his mother live well with our gold, our hen, and our harp. Jack says he took our things because we are mean, old giants. Well, that's not true. We were kind to that boy.

He had no right to take what was ours or to hurt my husband. Giants have feelings, you know. You wouldn't hurt a giant's feelings, would you?

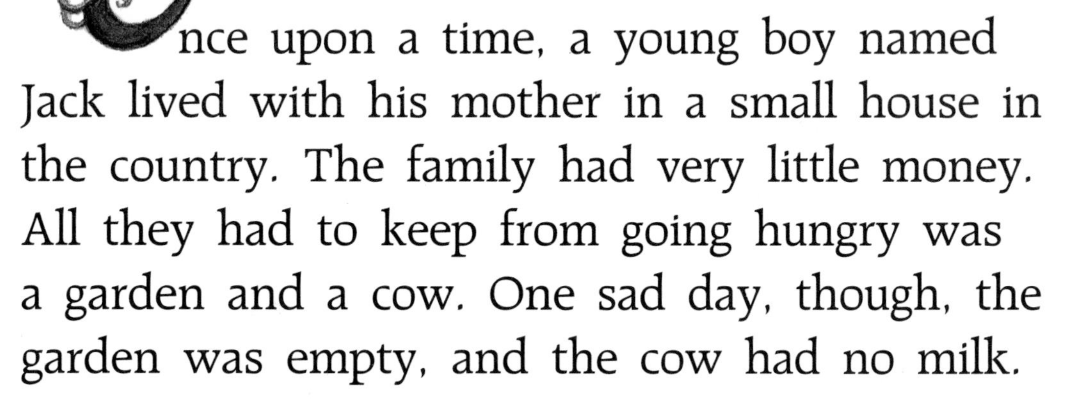

Once upon a time, a young boy named Jack lived with his mother in a small house in the country. The family had very little money. All they had to keep from going hungry was a garden and a cow. One sad day, though, the garden was empty, and the cow had no milk.

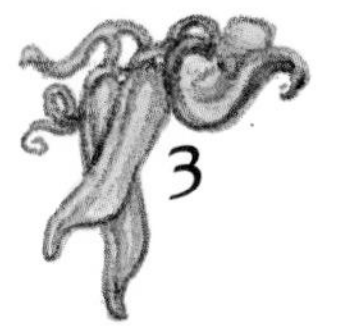

"Take the cow to market and sell her," said Jack's mother. "We will use the money to buy food."

Jack set off down the lane. He hadn't gone far when he came upon a stranger.

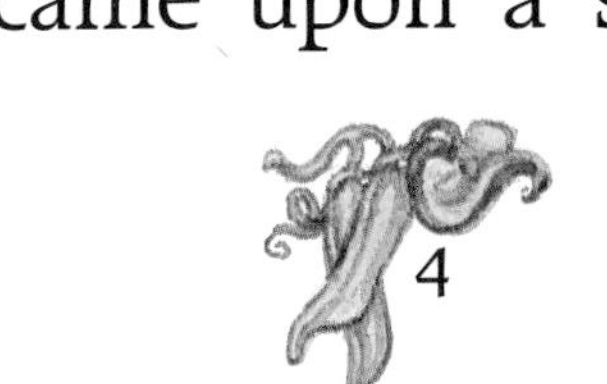

"I'm going to market to sell our cow," Jack said proudly.

"I can give you more than you'll get at market," the man said. "I'll give you some magic beans for that cow."

Jack thought that sounded like a very good deal. He traded the cow for the beans.

When Jack got home, his mother was not happy about what he had done. "How could you trade our cow for these beans?" she asked. "Now we shall surely starve!" With that, she threw the beans out the window.

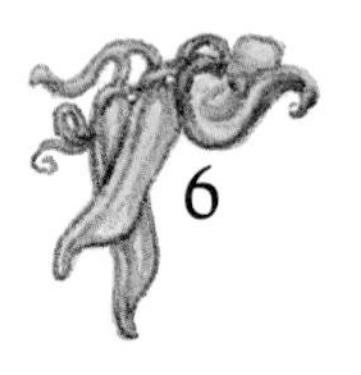

Since Jack brought home no money to buy food, both he and his mother went to bed without supper.

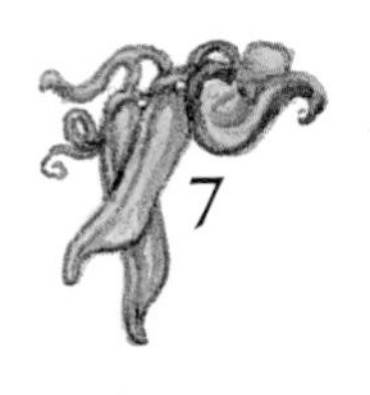

The next morning, Jack saw a tall shadow by the window. He peeked outside. A huge beanstalk stood where his mother had thrown the beans. The beanstalk was so tall that it went up into the clouds.

"Those were magic beans!" Jack cried. "No wonder there is a huge beanstalk." Jack wanted to see where the beanstalk went, so he climbed up and up. At the very top, he came to a road that led to a great stone castle. Jack didn't know that a mean giant lived there. He knocked at the door. A huge woman answered it, and Jack asked for something to eat.

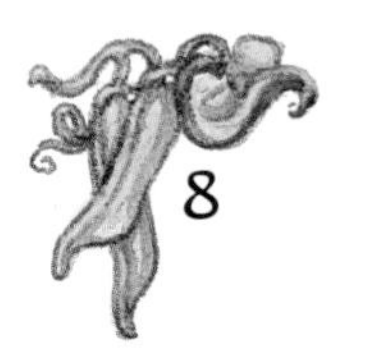

The woman was kind. She gave Jack some food. "You must be careful," she warned. "My husband is a giant. If he finds you, he will gobble you up. You must hurry and eat before he comes home."

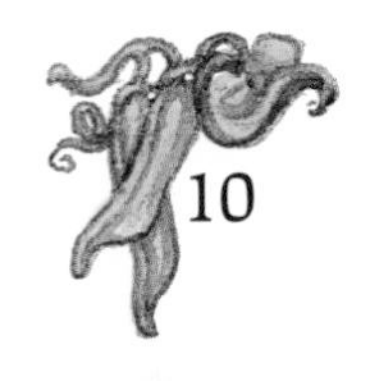

Just as Jack was about to finish the last crumb of bread, he felt the ground shake. "Quickly, hide in the oven," said the woman. Jack hopped into the oven.

The terrible giant stomped into the room and roared, "**Fe! Fi! Fo! Fum!** I smell the blood of an Englishman! Be he alive or be he dead, I'll grind his bones to make my bread!"

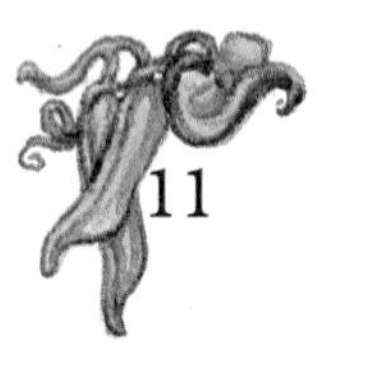

"It's just your breakfast you smell," said the woman. She brought the giant steaming hot bowls of food. He gulped them down.

"Bring me my gold!" the giant roared. So the woman brought two sacks of gold.

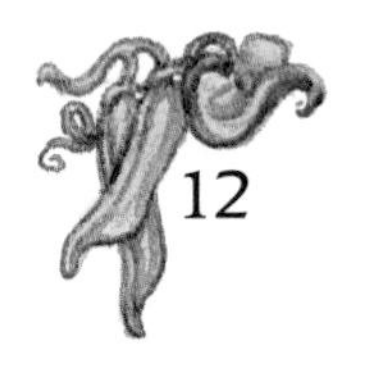

Jack's eyes grew wide as the giant counted the coins. "What that gold could buy for Mother and me!" he thought. Soon the giant's head was on the table. Loud snores shook the room. Jack saw his chance. He jumped from the oven and grabbed the gold.

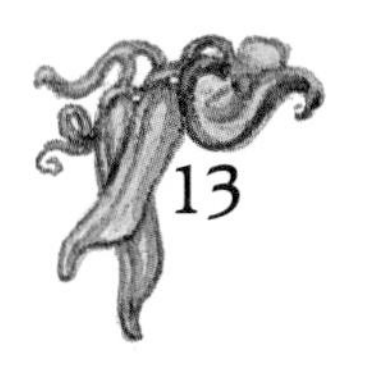

Jack ran to the beanstalk. Down he climbed. When he showed his mother the gold, she was very happy.

For a while, Jack and his mother lived well. But the day came when they had few coins left. Jack climbed the beanstalk again. Once more, he knocked at the door and asked the woman for something to eat.

Jack was just finishing his tea when the ground began to shake. He leaped into the oven to hide.

The terrible giant stomped into the room and roared, "**Fe! Fi! Fo! Fum!** I smell the blood of an Englishman! Be he alive or be he dead, I'll grind his bones to make my bread!"

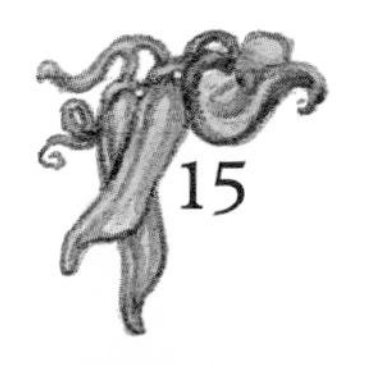

“What you smell is your dinner,” said the woman. The giant sat down, and his wife brought huge plates of food. When the giant gobbled up his meal, he yelled, “Bring me my hen!”

“Lay!” the giant roared to the hen. The hen laid an egg of gold. “Lay!” the giant shouted again. The hen laid another golden egg. Jack watched with wonder.

“What that gold could buy for Mother and me!” Jack thought.

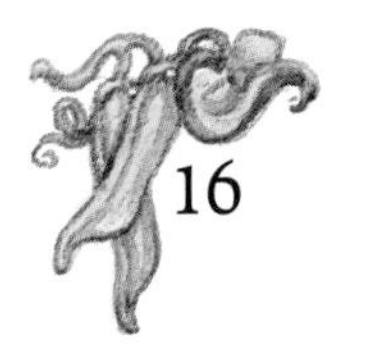

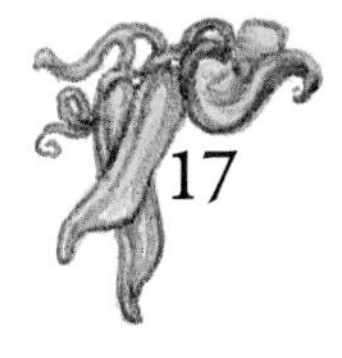

Soon, the giant's head was on the table. Loud snores shook the room.

Jack jumped from the oven and grabbed the hen. He ran to the beanstalk, and down he climbed. When he showed his mother the hen that laid golden eggs, she was very happy.

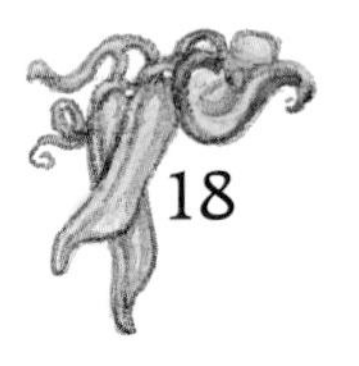

So for a while, Jack and his mother lived well from the hen's golden eggs. But the day came when Jack wanted more. He climbed the beanstalk again. This time he slipped into the castle without anyone seeing him. He popped into the oven to wait.

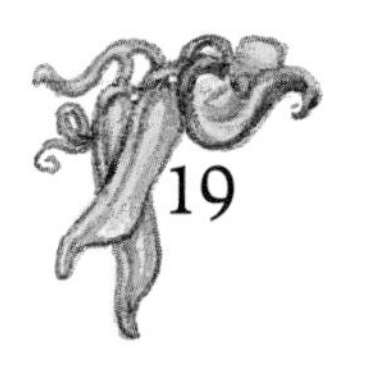

Soon the ground began to shake. The terrible giant stomped into the room and roared, "**Fe! Fi! Fo! Fum!** I smell the blood of an Englishman! Be he alive or be he dead, I'll grind his bones to make my bread!"

The giant's wife brought him boiling pots of food. He said no more about Englishmen. Soon he yelled for his golden harp. "Play!" the giant roared. Lovely music filled the room.

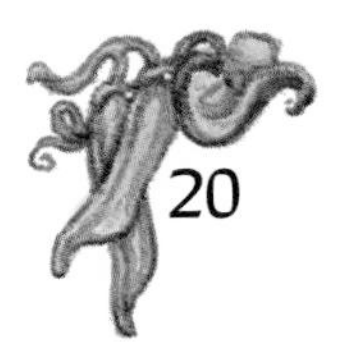

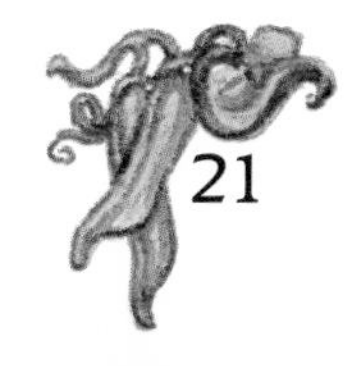

"I'd love to have that harp," Jack thought. So, when the giant's snores shook the room, Jack leaped from the oven and grabbed it.

As Jack raced to the beanstalk, the harp cried out, "Help, master!" The giant woke up with a roar and chased them. Jack was so scared, he nearly flew down the beanstalk. He screamed to his mother to get an ax. Jack quickly chopped away at the beanstalk. With a thud, the giant fell to the earth, crashing hard upon his head.

Jack and his mother, though, lived happily ever after with the gold, the hen, and the harp.

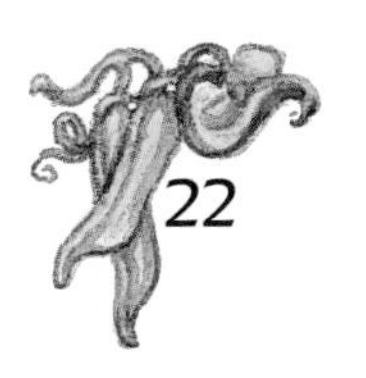